D0585756

Materials and characters from the movie *Cars 2*. Copyright © 2011 Disney/Pixar.
Disney/Pixar elements © Disney/Pixar, not including underlying vehicles owned
by third parties; and, if applicable:
Pacer and Gremlin are trademarks of Chrysler LLC;
Jeep® and the Jeep® grille design are registered trademarks of Chrysler LLC;
Porsche is a trademark of Porsche; Sarge's rank insignia design used with the approval
of the U.S. Army;
Volkswagen trademarks, design patents and copyrights are used with the approval of
the owner, Volkswagen AG;
Bentley is a trademark of Bentley Motors Limited;
FIAT is a trademark of FIAT S.p.A.;
Corvette, El Dorado, and Chevrolet Impala are trademarks of General Motors;
Background inspired by the Cadillac Ranch by Ant Farm
(Lord, Michels and Marquez) © 1974.

Published by Hachette Partworks Ltd
ISBN: 978-1-906965-54-9
Date of Printing: May 2011
Printed in Singapore by Tien Wah Press

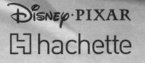

DISNEY · PIXAR

Cars 2

DISNEY · PIXAR

hachette

Secret agent Finn McMissile was on a mission. On an oil derrick hidden in the middle of the ocean, he was spying on the enemy: tiny green Professor Z and his thugs, some Gremlins and Pacers. They had crushed and cubed Finn's fellow agent. But Finn also had his eye on a TV camera with WGP on its side.

Why was that camera here?

Meanwhile, in Radiator Springs, Lightning, Sally and all their friends were at the restaurant. On TV, Francesco Bernoulli, the Italian racing car, challenged Lightning to race in the World Grand Prix – three races in Japan, Italy and England. Lightning accepted the dare: "I'm in! Ka-chow!!"

Mater was thrilled when Lightning decided to take him along for the races. Sir Miles Axlerod, the former oil baron, was the sponsor of the World Grand Prix. He started by hosting a big party in Tokyo.

Secretly, Finn and Agent Holley Shiftwell watched the party.

Axlerod was talking to Lightning about his new alternative fuel, Allinol. All the cars in his World Grand Prix would use Allinol. But during their conversation, Mater started leaking!

Horrified, Lightning told him to go to the bathroom to clean up his oil.

In the bathroom, Mater accidentally interrupted a fight between an American secret agent and two of Professor Z's thugs, Grem and Acer. The American agent, Rod, stuck a coded electronic device under Mater just before the rusty tow truck left the bathroom.

Agent Holley Shiftwell met Mater outside the bathroom. She picked up the signal from the device Rod had planted.

Naturally, Holley thought Mater was the American agent – and that he had top-secret information for her! She told him to meet her the next day at the first race.

Grem and Acer took Rod to Professor Z. The little green car found out Mater had the device. Now the tow truck was in trouble – big trouble!

"We've secretly sabotaged Axlerod's wonderfuel," Professor Z said, filling Rod with Allinol. Professor Z was working for someone with an evil agenda.

When the fake WGP camera sent out a radiation beam, the Allinol – and Rod – went *KA-BOOM*!

The next day at the race, Finn and Holley were looking for Mater. Finally, Holley spotted Mater with Lightning's pit crew.

Meanwhile, Professor Z had received a message from his "Big Boss". Now the Gremlins and Pacers were closing in on Mater, trying to get hold of Rod's device.

Holley had to protect Mater! She radioed him and told him to get out of the pit area.

Mater did as she asked. He thought Holley wanted to meet up with him!

Mater left the pit area and saw Finn fighting off the Gremlins and the Pacers. He talked to Holley on his radio, without realising that Lightning could hear too!

Lightning thought that Mater was giving him racing tips.

When Lightning followed Mater's "tips", Francesco zoomed past Lightning and won the race! Afterwards, Lightning confronted Mater.

"Why were you yelling things at me while I was racing?" he shouted. "I lost the race because of you!"

Mater felt terrible. He took off for the airport to go home.

He didn't know Grem and Acer were following him. Luckily, Holley and Finn saved him by sweeping him away in a secret-agent jet!

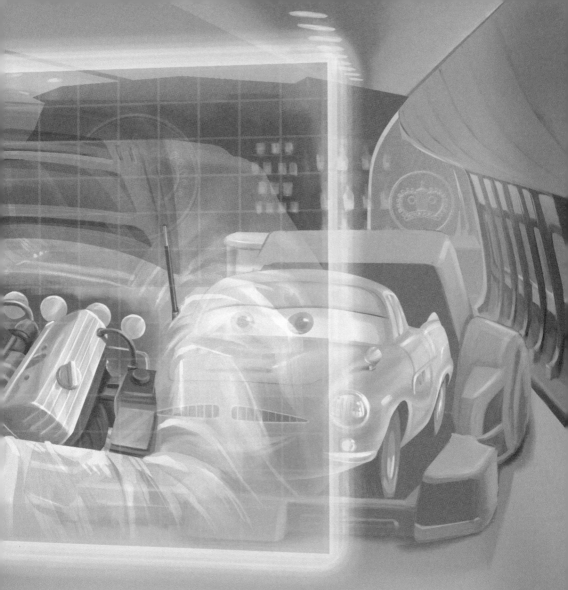

Holley retrieved the device from Mater. It contained just one photo: a mysterious engine. Finn was convinced that whoever owned this engine was behind the sabotage plot.

Mater noticed the engine had been modified, using expensive spare parts. Finn had an idea. If they found out where the parts came from, they could learn the identity of the engine's owner!

Soon, the three cars were in Paris with Tomber, a spare-parts dealer. Mater called the Big Boss a "Lemon" – a kind of car that didn't work properly. Professor Z and his thugs were also Lemons.

Tomber's headlights practically beamed!

"There have been rumours of a secret meeting of these so-called Lemon cars in two days," he said. The meeting was in Porto Corsa, Italy, near the next World Grand Prix race!

Wearing a high-tech disguise, Mater got into the Lemonheads' meeting. Professor Z arrived without Big Boss, who was being repaired. The Lemonheads understood. It was hard being a Lemon. They had to be repaired all the time.

The Big Boss's engine appeared on a TV screen. It was the same engine as the one in the photo!

The Big Boss spoke to the Lemons. The World Grand Prix was supposed to show off Allinol, the alternative fuel. But the Lemons owned the oil derricks. They *wanted* Allinol to look dangerous!

The Lemons were already targeting another racing car with the WGP camera! Finn and Holley heard this over Mater's radio and sped off to stop them.

But all too quickly, Finn, Holley and Mater were captured. The three were tied to the giant, crunching gears of a huge clock in London.

When Grem and Acer told Mater that they were going to destroy Lightning, Mater escaped and headed straight to Lightning's pit stop at the London race!

Holley and Finn escaped, too, but they discovered something terrible.

"Mater, listen to me!" Finn radioed. The enemy had placed a bomb on Mater! At Lightning's pit stop, Mater quickly raced away. He had to keep that bomb away from his friends!

Lightning didn't want Mater to leave, not again. They were best friends! Lightning was determined to apologize to Mater for getting angry with him in Tokyo. He attached himself to Mater's tow hook. As the Lemons closed in on Mater, Holley sped to help.

"Deactivate the bomb!" Finn shouted as he hauled in the evil Professor Z. But the bomb was voice-activated. The timer still ticked away.

"It can only be deactivated by the car who activated it," Professor Z said. That car must have been the Big Boss! But where — and who — was he?

All Mater's friends from Radiator Springs arrived to help fend off the Lemons. Guido tried to remove the bomb from Mater. But none of Guido's wrenches worked on the strange bolts.

And then Mater understood it all.

Mater activated his spy parachute and rockets, hooked Lightning to him, and flew to Buckingham Palace. The Queen and Miles Axlerod were there, waiting to greet the racers.

Mater glared at Axlerod. Mater had not leaked oil in Tokyo. He never leaked. The mysterious engine in the photo was Axlerod's. *He* was the Big Boss!

"He wanted to make Allinol look bad so everyone would go back to oil!" declared Mater. The bomb ticked down to two seconds.

"Deactivate!" Axlerod screamed. The bomb and the World Grand Prix stopped right then and there.

Mater was knighted by the Queen and became an international hero. Then he returned to Radiator Springs with his best buddy, Lightning McQueen.

The other international race cars joined them. Radiator Springs was now hosting the final race to find the fastest car in the world.

Finn and Holley arrived and asked Mater if he would accompany them on their next mission, but Mater said no.

"This is where I belong," he said, smiling at all his friends.

But Mater did ask them for one last favour: permission to use his secret-agent rockets.

Mater zoomed onto the track to join Lightning at the head of the race. The two best buddies were together again at last!